Puss - in - Boots

Retold by Vaijayanti Savant Tonpe

Illustrated by Utsav Bhattacharya

MSM PRESS

Once upon a time there was a miller who had three sons. The miller worked hard and provided enough for his family. But he owned only three things. They were his mill, a mule and a beautiful cat. When the miller died, his sons divided the three among themselves.

While the youngest son got the cat, the elder two took the mule and the mill.

The youngest son was very sad. He could not kill the cat and eat her flesh. But if he did he could make gloves out of her fur. Yet, what would he do after that? What would he eat? What would he live on?

His cat was very wise and clever. She knew her master was worried. She had a wonderful plan for him.

She said, "Get me a pair of boots and a coat. Then see how I change your life."

The young boy knew that his cat was clever. He also knew he had no plans of his own.

So he thought he would do as his cat asked him.

The boy got the cat a pair of boots and a hat. She put them on and walked up and down with pride.

Suddenly she ran off to the forest.

She chased a rabbit there, and tricked it into a trap.

The cat took the rabbit to the royal palace and said,

"I have a gift for His Majesty from the Duke of Carabas."

The cat was taken into the King's presence.
She offered the rabbit to him as a gift.
"How nice of your master, the Duke, to honour me with
this gift !" said the King patting the cat.

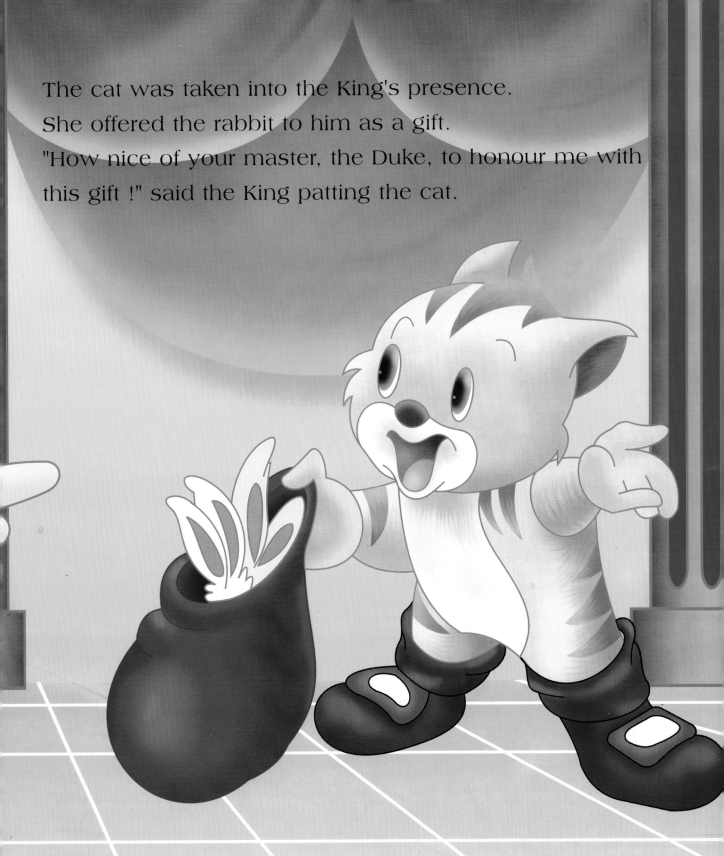

Next, the cat caught two wild pheasants. She presented them
to the King, The King took the birds and thanked the cat and his
master once again.

The cat returned to her master and both went to the countryside. The cat had come to know that the King, along with his beautiful daughter, was touring the countryside in a chariot.
"Master! Do as I ask and you'll never be sorry. Take off your clothes and jump into the lake."

The boy did not know what the cat was planning.

But he trusted her and did what she told him to do.
Soon they saw the royal chariot coming
towards them.
The cat hid the boy's clothes under a heavy rock.
"Help! Help!!
Thieves have thrown my master
into the lake and stolen his clothes.
Run, please, run to save my
master, the Duke. He is
drowning," shouted the
clever cat at the top of
her voice.

Hearing the cat's call, the King turned towards
the lake. He immediately recognised the cat who had
brought him many presents. He ordered his
coachman to help the Duke out of the lake.
He also told him to take fresh new clothes for him.

When the boy was rescued and
dressed, the King welcomed
him into his chariot with a smile.
The young boy sat in the chariot
with the King and his daughter
as he rode on.
The cat ran ahead
of them.

Soon the cat reached the castle of an ogre, who was known for his black magic.

She went in and said to the ogre, "Good Sir, I've come to see your magic with my own eyes. I have heard that you can change yourself into a mighty lion. Please, Sir, would you become a lion in front of my eyes?"

The ogre was highly flattered. He wasted no time and changed himself into a fearful lion.

Immediately the cat asked him to change into his original form. He did and the cat clapped for joy.

Then, clever as she was, she asked,
"Can you become a mouse, Sir?"
"Yes," said the ogre and he turned himself into a
mouse. The wise cat pounced on him and ate him up.

Just a few moments later, the King's chariot reached
the castle.
"Welcome, Your Majesty, to the Duke's castle,"
said the clever cat bowing low before the king.
The King and the Princess were very impressed by
the young man's riches.
The boy, was very proud of his beloved pet.

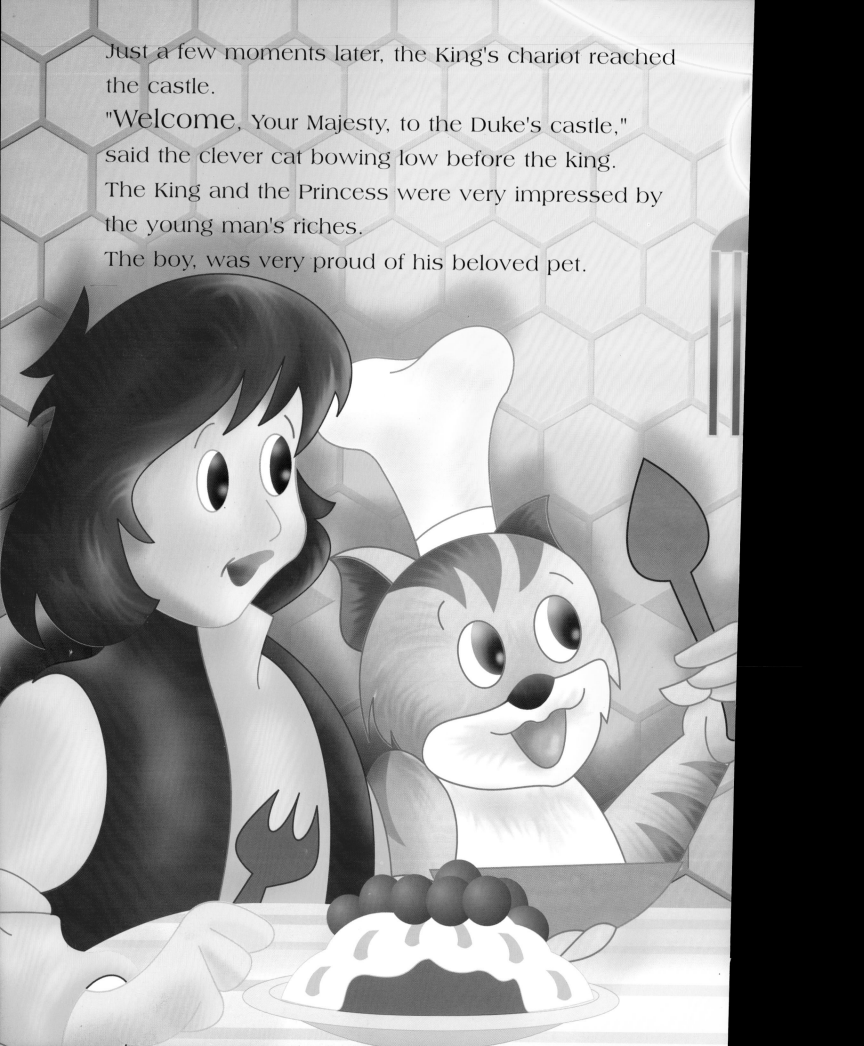

A rich feast was laid out before the King, but the Princess and the Duke could not stop talking to each other.

The King noticed this and decided they should marry each other.

As soon as the King went back to his palace the marriage of the Princess and the Duke was performed with royal fanfare.

The Duke and his bride were very happy.
But Puss-in-Boots was the happiest.
She had made the poor little boy with only
a cat into a future king. She could do so
because she was clever and loved her
master. Her master loved her too.

He and the Princess gave
Puss-in-Boots a special room
in the palace and looked after
her like their own child.